Little, Brown and Company

Hachette Book Group
1290 Avenue of the Americas, New York, NY 10104
Visit us at lb-kids.com
mylittlepony.com

LB kids is an imprint of Little, Brown and Company.
The LB kids name and logo are trademarks of Hachette Book Group, Inc.

The publisher is not responsible for websites (or their content) that are not owned by the publisher.

First Edition: July 2016

Library of Congress Control Number: 2016938028

ISBN 978-0-316-36150-7

10 9 8 7 6 5 4 3 2 1

PHX

Printed in the United States of America

Licensed By:

HAPPY HAUNTING

Adapted by Louise Alexander

Based on the episode
"Scare Master" by Natasha Levinger

LB kids

It was a dark and stormy night in Ponyville. Everypony's house was decorated with bats, skeletons, and pumpkins with spooky faces. Masked ponies roamed the streets.

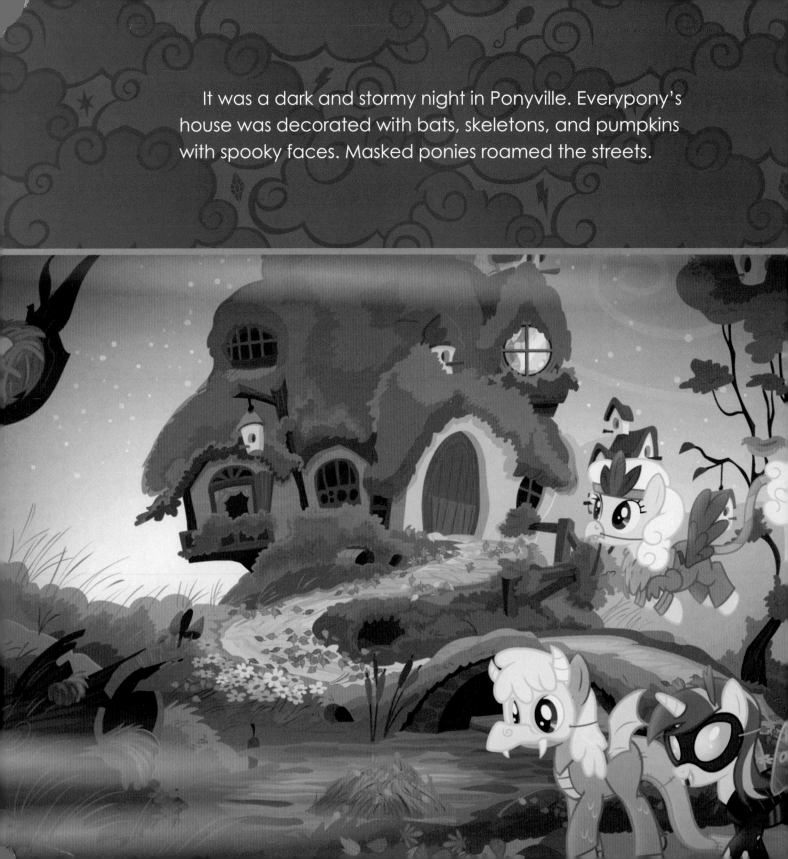

It wasn't just the wild winds that made Fluttershy shiver. Tonight
was her least favorite holiday of the year: Nightmare Night.

Outside her window, ponies sang:
"Nightmare Night!
What a fright!
Give me something good to bite!
If you don't,
I don't care,
But beware of a big, bad scare!"

Frights and bites and scares! How could anypony think
these things were fun? They were terrifying!

Fluttershy liked adorable things, particularly animals.
She did not like being frightened or startled.

So she had always spent
Nightmare Night hiding
under her bed. If she didn't
leave, there was no way
she could be scared!

This year, though, Fluttershy wanted to join her friends. As she walked through a long, dark hallway in the Castle of Friendship to meet the other ponies, she trembled.

Even though she was excited to share the holiday traditions with her friends, Fluttershy wondered what she was getting herself into!

When Fluttershy found the other ponies, they were posing and admiring the outfits they had picked.

Applejack was an adorably fierce lion. Rainbow Dash was ready for blastoff as a space pony. Twilight Sparkle looked golden as a gladiator. Pinkie Pie was letting the good times roll as a disco skater. Rarity shimmered as a beautiful mermaid.

"Fluttershy, it's your turn to choose a costume," Rarity encouraged. "It can be spooky, beautiful, or funny. Use your imagination!"

Fluttershy emerged from the closet in a simple black dress.

"*Ooh, you're a robber? A ninja?*" Pinkie Pie guessed.

"I'm the belle of the Masquerade Ball… without the mask, of course! This way if a ghost pony jumps out at me, I'll be able to spot it and make a quick escape!"

Soon it was time to teach Fluttershy some Nightmare Night games.
When Rainbow Dash began a round of Pin the Horn on Nightmare
Moon, Fluttershy passed. "If I'm blindfolded, I won't be able to see if
something spooky comes up behind me!"

Pinkie Pie didn't think there was any danger in bobbing for apples, but Fluttershy found an excuse. "Oh no! If my head is underwater, I won't be able to hear a monster roaring into the room!"

Each pony explained her favorite game, but Fluttershy found a reason to be afraid of *all* of them....

Pinkie Pie perked up and pulled out bags of treats for each pony. "There's nothing to fear about eating candy!"

"I don't know," Fluttershy said nervously. "It looks very gooey and chewy. What if my teeth stick together and I can't scream for help?"

Sensing that her friends wanted a fright, Fluttershy had an idea. "Meet at my house in one hour!"

As the ponies entered a dark, foggy room, Fluttershy called out in her best ghoulish voice, "Welcome to my haunted tea party. I hope you can handle it!"

The ponies looked at one another, excited that their friend was finally getting into the spooky spirit of the holiday.

As Applejack reached to pass the sugar, Fluttershy warned, "The sugar bowl is empty. You're a terrible host!"

Then she cackled at Pinkie Pie. "Offer the guest to your left a slice of cake."
Pinkie Pie looked confused. "But there's no one there!"
"Exactly! She canceled without even telling you."
Twilight Sparkle complained, "This isn't very scary!"

"Oh dear. No one finds bad party manners as terrifying as I do?" Fluttershy cried. "I thought it would be nice to spend Nightmare Night with my friends, but all I've done is ruin the fun. I'm not cut out for a night of frights. Go on to the corn maze without me."

She hung her head as her friends headed off to Applejack's farm.

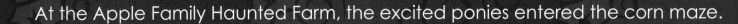

At the Apple Family Haunted Farm, the excited ponies entered the corn maze.

They laughed as Big Mac jumped out dressed as a mummy. "Booyup."
They squealed when their hooves crunched over sticks painted to look like bones, and they shuddered when they brushed against grapes hung like mushy eyeballs in a dark tunnel.

Suddenly, the corn rustled behind them. Three ghosts popped out and chased after the ponies. The ponies ran for an exit but took a wrong turn and tumbled down a hole.

Twilight Sparkle used her magic to light up the cave and spotted Granny Smith. As the ponies got closer, their relief turned to horror—it wasn't Granny, but a ghastly Granny Skeleton!

As they shook with shock, the ponies heard a *thump, thump, thump.*
The noise was getting closer. Seconds later, a cave monster towered
over them, roaring angrily.

The ponies bolted so fast, they didn't even see a giant spiderweb
in front of them. They became tangled in the stickiness.

"Th-this w-wasn't part of the maze Granny designed," Applejack
stuttered. "I'm really scared!"

The ponies broke free and sprinted down a tunnel into a field.

Just when they thought they were safe, a winged creature swooped out of the sky. The ponies screamed! It was a giant vampire fruit bat with sharp fangs and red eyes!

A full moon emerged from behind the clouds. In the light, the ponies saw it wasn't a bat after all. It was Fluttershy!

Their screams turned to cheers.

"I'm so sorry," Fluttershy apologized as she landed on the ground.
"I didn't mean to give you all such a fright!"

"Don't apologize, Fluttershy!" Pinkie Pie exclaimed.
"That. Was. AWESOME!"

"I had a little help from my friends." Fluttershy blushed as her animal friends gathered around and took off their costumes.

Birds flew through the maze as ghosts. Fuzzy Legs spun the web the ponies got stuck in, and Hairy the Bear was the giant cave monster.

"You did a great job scaring us, and I'm so proud of you." Rarity beamed. "We know how scary this holiday is for you, and it means a lot that you came out of hiding to experience Nightmare Night with us."

"Thanks, friends," Fluttershy said with confidence. "But I think this will be my first and last Nightmare Night."

As she hugged everypony, Fluttershy was happy that she had joined her friends. She also learned she wasn't a pony who enjoyed scaring other ponies or being scared. Her friends like it, but it just didn't feel right to her—and that was okay. There were plenty of other activities the ponies could enjoy together.

At the end of the night, Fluttershy got cozy in her fort, curled up with her animal friends, and opened the least scary book she could find.

"Now, this," she said, "is the perfect Nightmare Night."